EO WRITES

Penned with Purpose

Poetry

Contents

IV Enemies of God

V America

I

The Bride

Write About Me

Write about Me.
What should I say?
What should I write?
Write about ME with all of your might!
That they may hear and that they may have sight
of who I AM and what is right!

Purity

Who desires purity? God!
How do you obtain it?
By gaining Godly wisdom…through God's Word.

Purity is what I desire.
Purity is my fire.
Come with Me.
Come a little higher
for purity is what the King desires!

Hand-Picked

When I was despised in men's eyes,
heavily scrutinized, not accepted, always rejected.
You came along and heard my downcast song.
You picked me when no one else would agree.
For you saw in me what I could be with just one touch from thee.
It doesn't matter if I came tethered for you are fitting me for your endeavors.
In the end, the world will see the value you placed in me.
None will be able to disagree, for you are GOD and you yourself hand picked
me.

Taking Flight

Arrayed in splendor, so shall I be.
Adorned before my master for all to see.
All will gasp at the sight as the radiant bride takes flight.

A Restored Bride

Give her beauty for ashes,
joy for mourning.
May she be a beautiful tree
that stands strong for thee.
1

Knowing God

Knock, knock
Who's there?
Orange
Orange who?
Orange you glad you know Me?

A New Day

Red roses, red noses, and a whole lot of poses
as in the day of Moses.
For here we are not a distant star.
About to embrace a wonderful place
as the ground around us begins to quake
and God appears in the wake.
For God will have his way and in the end he will say make my day
as the enemy gives way to what he has to say!

All Things Through Christ

❧

I can do all things through Christ who strengthens me.
For you alone give us the victory.

II

Love

My Daddy

My daddy was a man of great strength and wit.
He knew the value of hard work and he wasn't one to quit.
He believed in God and his dear son and sang
of the victories he had already won.
He worked ever so faithfully with his hands
and kept his wedding vows to the end.
A father, a husband, a friend.
These are just a few of the titles given to men.
But when it comes to one's story end
may it be one who was "faithful" and
one who gave his all to Him.

2

Lessons From My Dad

I learned the importance of the Word by observing his unswerving
dedication
to its application.
I learned the importance of praise by God's grace
as he sang to God throughout his many days.
I learned the importance of hard work and dedication to one's occupation.
I learned the importance of vows as he stood with his spouse.
I learned the importance of laughter and the heart
felt medicine that comes after.
I learned the importance of sacrifice and that love makes all things right.

Date Ride

My husband and I head out for a ride
as night draws nigh.
Holding on tightly, I do not take lightly
the dangerous road we implore.
I trust, but once more;
that God will do what he has done before.
For he knows how to keep us
when the enemy's plans are to defeat us.
So with delight, we venture out into the twilight.
Knowing the Ancient of Days has us always in his gaze.

One

Two hearts
Two souls
One purpose
One goal
One voice
That all will know.

Two Castles, One King

Two castles, one King,
only one offers a ring.
To be the King of a vast domain
but not to have your Queen is quite insane.
Why would a man settle for two when his
precious is the one that said I do.

Time Bomb

Time is ticking yes in deed.
Is it time for you and me?
With Jesus two makes three.
Now it's time to deliver-
one, two, three!
Boom!
I told you it was time for Thee!

III

Reflection

You Are God, I Am Not

How often we think we know what is best
when it is God who gives us rest.
God who made creatures big and small
decides the outcome of them all.
When it comes to the test,
it is the Father who knows what is best.
Do we trust His care in all?
or do we crumble from the fall?

You are God; I am not.

3

Prayer

Open my eyes to see that it is better to pursue purity.
I ask Lord that you would give me the golden key
that leads to all you have for me- a life that is full of thee.
For you are what I need in this hour of need.

Egypt

Have I settled for a distant land?
Was this even in God's plan?
To live in a land of many gods,
to hear the banging of the raging gongs!
As the gods here are lifted up oh so high.
to take to flight like eagles on high.
Is this what God intended for me?
Is this his reality?
How do I escape this land I am in?
I'm not even sure just where to begin.
I just know I need to find Him!
I have read the story of the promise land
and I look to Him to lend me a hand.
Is this the only way to escape this land I'm in?
When will He come and set me free?
So that I can truly be what He called me to be.
To rise above the distant fog, to see just where
I truly belong.
I hold on to His promise of the great land that
will be my promise land!
Come quickly LORD!

4

Promises

What did you see that night?
that gave you such a fright?
The winds blowing,
the chills up my spine,
as death intertwined.
Cold and empty was the house
that once gave life to all about.
I left, not knowing where to turn.
but my promises were what I yearned.
I returned once again,
for I needed to make amends.
In the end, forgiveness became my friend.
as I said goodbye to what was once alive.
As I reached for that door once more,
the doorknob fell to ash to the floor.
What was once my childhood home,
was gone and now I was alone.
O' death, where is your sting?
Now it is time to sing!
As I left death that time,
I heard a voice from behind —

My promises for you are grand,
now it is time for Me to open my hand!
Your journey has been long,
and those you loved are now gone.
It has not always been great, but it is time to celebrate!

5

Seasons

Seasons come, seasons go.
You need to know when to let go.
For God is a God in the know.
Turn to him from whom all blessings flow
and then let go!

Jesus

Jesus!
You are faithful, and you are true.
You know exactly what to do!
Why do I wrestle?
Why do I fret?
When it is not over yet.
You came from heaven up above
to fill our hearts with your vast love.
We must not let man tempt us with evil pleasures,
for what we have in him is such a magnificent treasure.

Joy

Over the mountains, and over the seas.
Tiny cottages, and mansions with vast histories.
Possible dangers as far as the eye can see,
do not let it rob you of your victories.
When fear appears, hold on to what is dear.
Stand strong, stand tall, stand above them all.
You will see that he stands ready to conquer all.
When the clock chimes and it is your time,
the joy you will find when you leave fear
far, far behind.

6

At the Crossroads

I've been at the crossroads from which you now stand.
Love isn't always easy, and it's not always grand.
But know that the Father is there holding your hand
and know that he knows where you now stand.
He loves you and accepts you no matter where you
chose to stand for he is the great I AM!

Will the True Church Please Stand Up

O Lord God, I beseech thee.
Are we really walking in victory?
Have we given up on the fight?
Have we forgotten what is truly right?
O Lord God, as you call out tenderly
What is it that you see?
As I venture on this flight on eagles' wings
enabled by your might.
Have we given ourselves to the night?
I ask as I grab hold of you with all my might.
O Lord God, I beseech thee.
Have we, Lord, strayed from your hand in this day?
The hour is late; the lights grow dim.
I find it hard to see him in this church I once walked in.
O Lord God, I beseech thee.
Where are you? my spirit cries as I look with wandering eyes
at the church around my eyes and then I hear you reply...
"I do not recognize" as the tears flow from my eyes.
What have we become? Have we become undone?
Have we forgotten thee?
For God desires purity, that is his reality!

O Lord God, I beseech thee.
For if purity isn't the thing indeed that is driving the church,
then what is it that be but a Christ-less church without
dignity, that is the true reality!
For without dignity we cease to be all that you called us to be!
For we are to stand for truth for all to see, no matter
what may come.
For all to see that it is Christ in us, the hope of glory for this
declares your majesty!
For all to see the hope of glory for this declares your majesty!

Soaring

A soaring eagle looking for a home.
Ten weeks and no church home.
Where is this lonesome bird going to perch?
I visited a Baptist church and found myself
not in a lurch.
The Savior was there, ready to greet me
for he knows how to keep me.
As we came in to praise him, I felt a hear felt
"at home" peace a blazing.
The Pastor spoke of a father's love, then of the
father from up above.
I felt right then a touch from him and knew I'd
never be the same again.
A few days later, a welcome gift came to my haven
by hand of the Pastor straight from the hand of the
master to a gentleman and his maiden addressed
from your friends at the Baptist church.
I am not at a lurch for God told me to visit this church.
Where is this lonesome bird going to perch?
Is this going to be my - home church?

God's Handmaiden

Favor is deceitful, and beauty is vain:
but a woman who fears the Lord she shall
remain.
Steady and strong for she knows where she belongs
and has a most precious song.

Although men threat they haven't seen anything yet.
For the hour is fast spent and God will not relent
and there will be a great upset.

Give her the fruit of her hands- her promise land
for this is God's glorious plan.
Watch how it ends because of Him as though
it never began.

God will have the final laugh.

7

Write Your Story

Write your story for God's glory.
For it's the only way to go, to bring about
such a beautiful delight to the one that watches
over you, you know.
For he is there offering a chair in glory, you know.
For your story is heaven's great glory for the lost souls
on the road that will come to the Father in that hour
because of the story you told.

Rose

I feel like a rose buried underneath the snow.
Waiting for the Son's effervescent warm glow.

IV

Enemies of God

Mock

They laughed
They cheered
They mocked
They smeared
Then God Almighty appeared.

8

Trust in Position

You trusted in your position to save you
now your position will unclaim you.
For you did not look to the King above
but gave into an unsaturated love
for power and gold you did what you were told
and didn't see the story that was about to unfold.
For why would a man give up his soul for something
he would never hold?
Now the time has come when men are on the run.
For God is about to come and they are the ones
that will be undone.
We the victors are about to have fun as God takes back
the positions that were won!

Haman's Fall

[9]Let the Haman's fall, once and for all.
For the lots they cast shall now be their own forecast.
For they didn't realize the plots they schemed would
be the ones that would kill their dreams.
For they were not for the American dream, their plan
was to cut America off at the knees.
For then they would have all their dreams.

Dollars & Sense

Dollars and cents was the name of the game
when your love was only gain.
Did you forget you can't take it with?
Were you afraid that it was to much to give?
As the word of God implies and you failed
to recognize- do not touch the apple of my eye.
For dollars and cents you thought it made sense
to touch that which was not yours and for that He
is coming for yours!

Do Not Touch My Prophet's

Touch a Prophet you who lack respect
and see what you get for you haven't seen
anything yet.
Appointing kings, casting crowns and turning
the world upside down.
What a mess, what a feast, for you unleashed
a ravenous beast.
That's about to sit in your seat for a glorious
feast.

10

The Wicked Castle

I don't care how many years they have been around.
They are about to go down for the truth that will be found.
Round and round they went in a tireless vent
until they were spent.
Around a castle that was not theirs hoping to
become its only heirs.
Causing many tares not realizing it would come back on theirs.
For they are the ones who will lose their hairs.

One Story

One story to end them all.
One story to cause a great fall.
For they thought they had it all
for pride comes before a fall.
However, there is one story
that is about to give God glory
that will expose them all.

11

Wide Open

They have a past they are trying to hide
but there is no where they can hide.
For you Lord are opening those doors wide.
You are going to open the doors wide for
all to see what they did to you and me.

12

Excavation

The time has come to end the percolation
for a vast excavation for there has been a miscalculation
with their observation for they tried a cancellation with
their manipulation & contamination for that there will
be an execution upon their plans and much humiliation.

O' Wicked Tree

O' wicked tree, O' wicked tree
how ugly are your branches.
You thought you had the victory
as you made your advances.
You will be pulled up aggressively
for you have no more chances.
O' wicked tree, O' wicked tree you
will watch as the right with God's
help advances.

Buh, bye!

13

Summer & Fall

Summer is over, fall has begun
but not the fall as in season but the fall of them
who without reason committed treason.
Treason against a land so grand in hopes of a lucrative hand.

V

America

Dreams

As you reach for your dreams,
"remember" those who gave
wind to your wings.

A Place For You

There's a place for you.
Wherever you see the stars,
the red, the white, and the blue
know there is a place for you.

Traveler

As I travel on this road of life.
May I face it with much delight.
As I view the stars so bright,
help me to keep my eyes on you
the true light that is so bright.
For you are the compass that
guides me in what's right.

Blown Away

They will be blown away
at what they thought they HAD
they did not have!

14

Crown

Crown one, crown two, why look at you.
Now what are you going to do as all eyes
are fixed upon you?
For it is time to be true to those entrusted to you
for there is much to do.
For there is an urgent matter, in which we must gather
to end the chatter of a political, social, and spiritual matter
that will cause many to scatter as their world shatters.

Final Wake Up Call

God is good, God is great.
There is no time to capitulate.
Now God will set the record straight
by correcting the imbalanced weight.
Doing this will cause the land to quake
as both sides begin to shake, causing
the scales to break at the great WEIGHT.
15

God's Glorious Entrance

God's glory for all to see,
for we gain the victory
as He comes on the scene
triumphantly for you and me.

He hasn't forgotten his promises
and He will amaze even the doubting Thomases.
Come one, come all, they are all about to fall.
Everyone is about to be in awe as God takes
center stage before all.

16

A Winter Glow

Glistening upon the snow was the beautiful winter glow
of a bride, so beautiful.
Arrayed in gold threads and covered with the flag of old
a true beauty to behold.
A lost covenant found again and to that, a great amen.
Old glory was her name and we will never be the same,
for we have taken hold of our claim and now have much to gain.

Forty Five

A President, a resident, why were so many hesitant?
A David, a father, and to some he was a bother.
He stood, he voiced, and too many they had no choice,
for they knew with him was the end of all of them. So,
with their venomous tongue and thieving hands,
they tried to break the land free of him.
However, they were never going to get an amen
for God stands with him.

Egg On the Wall

There once was a story about an egg
who sat on a wall and had a great fall.
To think how absurd, that one would
believe such a word that an egg that
had so misbehaved would not become
prey to them, which he betrayed.

Forty Seven

A voice was heard across the land,
men, and women in one accord voting for him.
For the people declared, change is in the air.
For they no longer wanted the tyranny that had
been there.
The people's house had become a place for weasels,
rats, and such and not about us.
As 2025, comes into view, we can rest assure God
knows what to do.

Fire & Ice

Underneath the snow stirs a beautiful amberous glow.
What it is nobody knows.
However, it is beginning to grow.

One would say fire and ice don't play nice and that
there is no way they can compromise.
But this my friend, has to do with Christ.
A burial, a mural, and now a quincentennial.

17

Notes

A RESTORED BRIDE

1

    To appoint unto them that mourn in Zion, to give unto them beauty for ashes,
    the oil of joy for mourning, the garment of praise for the spirit of heaviness; that they might
    be called trees of righteousness, the planting of the Lord, that
    he might be glorified. Isaiah 61:3

MY DADDY

2

    My daddy passed away on June 14,2018.
    I miss him dearly.

YOU ARE GOD, I AM NOT

3   Know ye that the Lord he is God: it is he that hath made us,
    and not we ourselves; we are his people, and the sheep of his pasture.
    Psalm 100:3

EGYPT

4   This poem was written before 2016 and here we are in 2024 and the great Exodus is upon us.

    Make America great again LORD!

PROMISES

5

    This poem is based on the wrestling of an adult child and her
    parents. Afraid that her parent's failings would nullify God's
    promises for her life she stepped away from them for a season.
    In that year long season God worked on her heart and her parents.

JOY

6   O taste and see that the Lord is good: blessed is the man that trusteth in him. Psalm 34:8

GOD'S HANDMAIDEN

7   <u>Inspiration:</u>
Proverbs 31:30,31
Psalm 2:4

MOCK

8   It's not over yet. It is just beginning!

Dearly beloved, avenge not yourselves, but rather give place unto wrath: for it is written, Vengeance is mine; I will repay, saith the Lord. Romans 12:19

HAMAN'S FALL

9   The lot is cast into the lap;
but the whole disposing thereof
is of the LORD.
Proverbs 16:33

DO NOT TOUCH MY PROPHET'S

10   And he changeth the times and the seasons: he removeth kings, and setteth up kings: he giveth wisdom unto the wise, and knowledge to them that know understanding:
Daniel 2:21

ONE STORY

11   <u>Inspiration:</u>
Pride goeth before destruction, and an haughty spirit before a fall.
Proverbs 16:18

WIDE OPEN

12   God's coming to "we the people's" defense.
Hold the line.

O' WICKED TREE

13   <u>Inspiration:</u>
O' Christmas Tree
Isaiah 18:5

BLOWN AWAY

14 **Note:**
President Donald J. Trump and America
Make America great again LORD!

FINAL WAKE UP CALL

15 TEKEL, though art weighed in the balances, and art found wanting.
Daniel 5:27

A just weight and balance are the LORD'S: all the weights of the bag are his work.
Proverbs 16:11

GOD'S GLORIOUS ENTRANCE

16 <u>Inspiration:</u>
"Step out of the traffic! Take a long,
loving look at me, your High God,
above politics, above everything."
Psalm 46:10 (MSG)

FIRE & ICE

17 When God brought quin centennial to me I did some research on what happened in history
500 years ago. It kept coming to me the Bible so I got out my Rose Book of Bible Charts,
Maps & Time lines to look at "How We Got the Bible" and found a gem.

From Rose Book of Bible Charts, Maps and Time Lines by Rose Publishing, 2017
    William Tyndale, a priest and Oxford scholar, translates the New Testament from Greek
(1525), but cannot get approval to publish it in England. He moves to Germany and prints
Bibles, smuggling them into England in sacks of corn and flour. In 1535 he publishes a part
of the Old Testament translated from Hebrew. In 1536, Tyndale is strangled and burned at
the stake. His final words are "Lord, open the King of England's eyes."
Tyndale is called the "Father of the English Bible" because his translation
forms the basis of the King James Version. Much of the style and vocabulary
we know as "biblical English" is traceable to his work.

God is revisiting history, the fire of God is on it's way!

About the Author

Lizzy has been married for 27 years. She and her husband enjoy traveling throughout the United States on their Harley-Davidson motorcycle.

Her passion is sharing God's love through her art and writing.

She hopes to get My ABC's & God, and I Am Special published in 2025.

"Never judge a book by its cover. What you find inside the pages might surprise you."

Note from the Author:

"A word fitly spoken is like apples of gold in pictures of silver."

Proverbs 25:11

If you have enjoyed this book, would you consider reviewing it on Amazon.com?

Thank you!

You can connect with me on:

- https://www.eowrites.com
- https://www.linkedin.com/in/elizabetho
- https://truthsocial.com/@Lizzywrites

Subscribe to my newsletter:

- https://www.subscribepage.io/write4him

Also by EO Writes

For who hath despised the day of small things? for they shall rejoice, and shall see the plummet in the hand of Zerubbabel with those seven; they are the eyes of the Lord, which run to and fro through the whole earth. Zechariah 4:10

A Case of Mistaken Identity

"Have you ever felt like the entire world was against you? In a case of mistaken identity, Sadie feels this way as a court trial challenges her deserving of a happy ending. Participants from both sides of the political spectrum are testifying in this pivotal court case, as her reputation is at stake. Those against her are claiming she is undeserving of her purpose. Is Judge Justice going to clear her of all accusations and give her a chance to start anew? In order to move forward with confidence, she needs to redeem her past."

https://www.amazon.com/dp/B0DP81PJGW

www.ingramcontent.com/pod-product-compliance
Lightning Source LLC
Chambersburg PA
CBHW072043170626
46811CB00008B/3142